Seymour Slug Starts School

BY CAREY ARMSTRONG-ELLIS

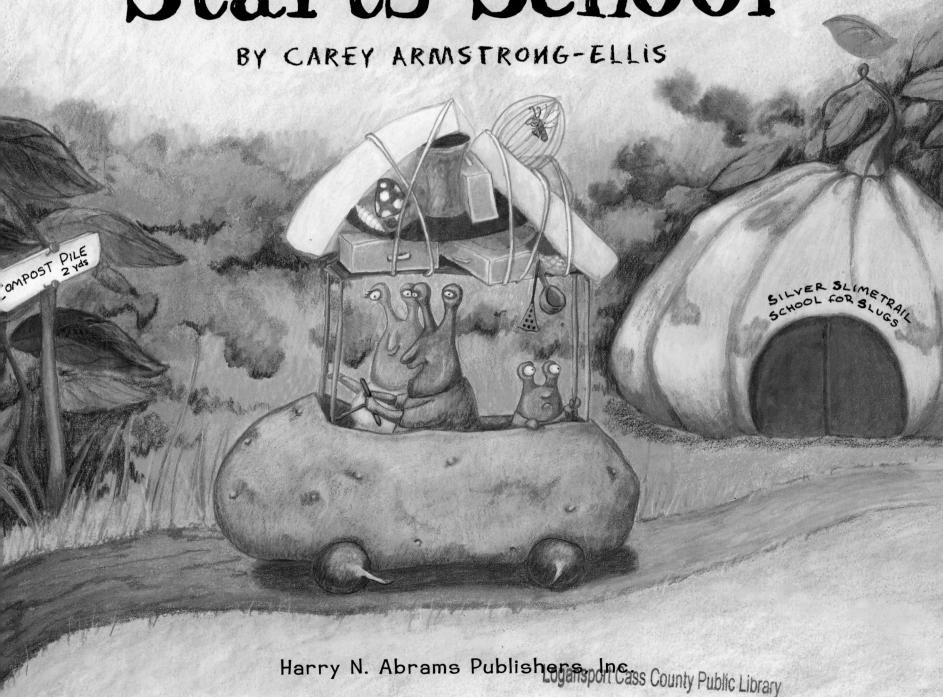

COMPOST PILE
2 Yds

SILVER SLIMETRAIL
SCHOOL FOR SLUGS

Harry N. Abrams Publishers, Inc.

Little Seymour gazed glumly out his bedroom window. He and his family had recently moved to their new home near the compost pile, and tomorrow was the first day of Slug School.

"I don't want to go," he thought. "What if nobody likes me? I bet everybody else can spell their names. I can't! And what if they play dodgeball? Or jump rope? I'm no good at dodging or jumping . . ."

With gloomy visions filling his head, he slithered into bed and pulled the blankets up over his face.

"Do not fear, little one!"

Seymour opened his eyes and beheld a wondrous sight. A beautiful fairy was hovering in the air before him.

"Wh-who are you?" he stammered.

"I am your Fairy Slugmother!" she said. "I am here to help you through any trouble you might have at school. So fret no more, for I, your Fairy Slugmother, will show you the way! Now get some sleep, you've a big day ahead of you."

And with that, she **poofed** out of sight.

The next morning Seymour woke up,
slid out of bed, and looked in the mirror.
"OK, I can do this," he told himself. "My
Fairy Slugmother will be there to help me."

At breakfast Seymour's mother said, "You seem chipper this morning. Have you changed your mind about school?"

"Yes, Mommy, because my Fairy Slugmother is going to help me!"

His mother smiled and said, "I'm glad you're feeling better—I'm sure you'll do just fine. Now eat up, I've fixed your favorite—toast with toadstool jam!"

The closer Seymour got to school, however, the more the feeling of dread seeped back. He thought of his Fairy Slugmother and crept on.
"She'll be there. It will be OK," he kept repeating.

When he arrived, he peeked around the door into the classroom.
"Hello, you must be Seymour," said the teacher. "Come in!" She
had a nice smile.
He slithered slowly into the room and sat down.

"Welcome, children," she said. "My name is Ms. Mildew. Our first project today is writing our names."

"Oh, no," groaned Seymour.

"You all have paper and pencils, and your names are written there at your tables—give it a try!"

"I can't do this," Seymour murmured to himself.

"Never fear!" cried the Fairy Slugmother as she popped up next to him. She grabbed the pencil and started to write. "But really," she considered, "this is dull, don't you think? Let's draw pictures instead!"

"No, no," whispered poor Seymour as he watched the Fairy Slugmother scribbling madly over paper after paper.

"That's imaginative, Seymour," Ms. Mildew said, smiling. "But why don't you try writing 'Seymour' now? I'm sure you can do it!"

"OK," Seymour said, sheepishly ducking his eyestalks. "I'm sorry. I'll try." He picked up his pencil and set to work. When he had finished, he looked nervously up at Ms. Mildew.

"That is excellent, Seymour! I knew you could do it,"
she said.

"Now we're going to plant lima beans," said Ms. Mildew, "and throughout the coming weeks we will watch them grow. When the beans are ready to pick, we will make lima bean cupcakes! Everyone please come to the front, put some dirt in a cup, and get a bean out of this jar."

The children slid forward.

"Uh-oh," worried Seymour, "what if I drop the jar and the beans go all over the floor? What if I spill the dirt?"

"I'll handle it!" shouted the Fairy Slugmother. She shot forward like a slick arrow, grabbed a scoop, and began tossing dirt into a cup. And into the air, onto the table, and onto the floor . . .

"Stop, stop!" whispered Seymour, furtively brushing dirt off a pile of papers.

"Why, Seymour!" exclaimed Ms. Mildew. "Why don't we sweep this up, and then you can try to fill your cup a little more carefully."

"Sorry," muttered Seymour. As he and Ms. Mildew started sweeping, Seymour sneaked a peek around the room. "I guess I'm not doing any worse than the other kids," he said to himself.

After the children had planted and watered their lima beans, Ms. Mildew announced that it was time for recess. They excitedly oozed out onto the playground. Seymour hung back, waving his eyestalks in distress.

"Maybe I should run away now, before I humiliate myself," he thought desperately. "I'll join the Cirque du Slug. They surely must need someone to sweep up the moldy popcorn . . ."

"Hey, Seymour!" Enid called. "Come over and jump rope!"

"I'll help you!" shrieked the Fairy Slugmother. She jabbed Seymour with her wand and he yelped and jumped. The jumprope caught him across the middle and he fell flat on his face. He just knew that everyone was laughing at him. He curled up in a ball and thought miserably, "Maybe if I stay perfectly still they will forget about me."

"Seymour?" Seymour looked up and saw Fred leaning over him. "You OK?"

"I guess so," said Seymour, slowly rising. He looked around. The other kids were not laughing at him at all!

"Well, come on then—let's play!" Fred said. Seymour grinned.

As Seymour started to join his classmates, the Fairy Slugmother fluttered forward. "I'll help you out!" she announced.

Seymour grabbed her skirt as she went
by. "You know, I think I'll take it from here."
   "Are you sure?" she asked doubtfully.
   "Yeah, I think I'll manage," he replied.
   "Hmm . . . OK, but call me if you need me!"
And she vanished, leaving nothing but
a wisp of sickly green vapor.

The rest of the day went swimmingly. They counted toadstool spores and painted pictures. Seymour shared his jellied turnip sandwich with his new friends.

When he got home, his mommy gave him a big hug. "How was your first day of school?" she asked.

"Great!" he said, then added, "Well, once the Fairy Slugmother left, that is . . ."

As he snuggled down in bed that night, once again the Fairy Slugmother popped up. "Will you be requiring my services tomorrow?" she asked hopefully.

"You know, I think I will be fine on my own," he replied. "School was actually fun!"

"I guess my work here is done," the Fairy Slugmother sighed. "But if you ever need me again, I'll be waiting!" She winked at him and faded from sight. As Seymour floated away to dreamland, he was confident that he could handle whatever school might have in store for him tomorrow.

Even dodgeball.